Gundaga Island

Lizanne Holland

authorHOUSE®

AuthorHouse™ LLC
1663 Liberty Drive
Bloomington, IN 47403
www.authorhouse.com
Phone: 1-800-839-8640

Published by AuthorHouse 01/14/2014

ISBN: 978-1-4918-5120-3 (sc)
ISBN: 978-1-4918-5119-7 (e)

Library of Congress Control Number: 2014900677

CONTENTS

In memory of my dear Jeff.
Gone Fishing.

Dedicated to my eleven grandchildren

To the memory of
Babe the dog, Woof.

Maddie, you were my inspiration thank you so much sweetheart.

GUNDAGA ISLAND

Here we come . . . .

CHAPTER ONE

IT WAS ALMOST SUMMERTIME AGAIN and the eleven cousins were looking forward to getting together again for an adventurous time. In actuality we should say the seven cousins because the twins now aged two being far too young and Camden and Makenzie aged six and four would find it difficult to keep up with the faster pace of the older ones. Their grand mother Gran Lizie although they all just call her Lizie lives on the shores of Gundaga beach in a cute little stone cottage overlooking the sea and Gundaga Island. The island is not too far away and can easily be reached by boat over the shallower spanse of water which would take around fifteen minutes and once there the rocky inlets and caves would await to be explored.

"Yes" shouted Christian the eldest of the eleven. "No more homework for a good two months" his blue green eyes dancing with glee.

"Mom, when shall we start packing our things?" asked Cole.

"Well I should say chirped in Caleb right now as tomorrow we are going to Gran Lizies' place for two whole weeks." Mom agreed that now was a good time to get their things together ready for an early start in the morning.

"Bother" said Catrin, "I cannot find my favorite pink shorts, mom have you seen them?"

"I thought that I had put them in your room Catrin, go and look again honey" said her mom. So they busily carried on stuffing their canvas bags to the brims, most importantly not forgetting the bathers. Camden the youngest of the five C's had packed his bag but not with clothes but his favorite toys!

"Camden you need to re-pack that bag, you play with toys not wear them" said Caleb. Camden sulked at his older more serious brother but did as he was told. Meanwhile at Sam and Abbeys' house much the same was going on packing up and exciting chatter about their up-coming vacation.

"Hey Sam, do you think that we will have some good adventures at Lizies' place?"

"Think so said her brother, I think that if we can find an old row boat we could plan to go out to Gundaga Island to explore."

"Gosh Sam that sounds so exciting and to be with our cousins too."

With very active thoughts the two of them continued to pack up their things.

"I wonder how Maddie and Kenzies' packing is coming along, shall we call them Sam?" asked Abbey.

"Better not until everything is done here he said, then we can call them."

"You're right replied Abbey, oh I do love having an older brother like you Sam."

"Time for supper you two up there, it's pepperoni pizza your favorite" shouted their mom. So with that they both raced down the stairs as kids do to see who would get to the dinner table first.

"Mom asked Sam, can we call Maddie and Kenzie when we have eaten?"

"Sure you can said their mom, I hope that they are all packed up by now as you two have done, good job kids."

"Yes said their dad, I think that you have remembered everything even the life jackets." Sam and Caleb are both eleven and make a good team together.

"I need to call Caleb too said Sam but first let's call Maddie and Kenzie" he said to Abbey.

"Well are you all ready for an exciting two weeks at Lizies' place? Sam asked his cousins.

"You bet was the reply, I can hardly wait to see Gundaga beach, Lizies' cottage as it's the best and of course our dear Lizie."

"Madison do you have all your things together?" asked her mom.

"Yep replied Maddie, and I am about to bring my bag down to put at the front door." Oh musn't forget my i-pod too she thought . . . .

"Mommy shouted Kenzie, do I need my sweaters for the trip?"

"No dear you don't."

Now let me see thought the little girl, I will need my Santa doll, my fish and my good-night book which sings lullabyes to me and with that she stuffed them all into her gaily colored bag.

Kenzie hopes to spend alot of her time on Gundaga beach with Lizie and Camden digging around in the sand finding colorful shells to add to her collection.

"Kenzie it is summertime almost and we only wear sweaters in the winter."

"OK, I get it" and continued to mess around in her room instead of zipping up her bag and placing it at the top of the stairs. Eventually it would end up at the front door with Maddies' when mom had a moment.

The next morning dawned at around six and looked to be a warm late spring day in early June. The smell of bacon, eggs and hash browns filtered through the kitchen of the five C's and the twins' place and as usual they were all more than ready to tuck in with lashings of orange juice and milk.

"How long will it take us to get to Gundaga?" asked Cole.

"Oh about an hour and a half" replied his mom as she quickly cleared up the breakfast dishes. "Boys can you load up the van" she also asked, then we can be on our way."

"Consider it done" was the echo of the three older boys coming through the doorway loud and clear, "We should be able to leave soon."

Moments later all clambered into their seats ready for the drive which would be quite nice going through the country.

The same was taking place at the other cousins' houses, SUV's loaded up and ready to leave.

"I wonder who will get there first remarked Maddie, or do you think that we will all arrive at the same time?"

"Well we only have an hours' drive to Gundaga as do Sam and Abbey so we'll just have to see" mom added.

Babe the dog began to woof at all the comings and goings at Sam and Abbeys' house.

"Can Babe come along for the ride?" asked Abbey.

"Sure thing" said their dad.

"Here Babe jump up into the back as she lifted the back hatch up, and settle down" she said to the over excited dog. "We don't want dad to change his mind now do we."

Woof he went again woof!

The sun was climbing higher into the sky as all three vehicles made their way east to Gundaga. Very soon the kids' eyes would be scanning the horizon over the sea and out to Gundaga Island.

Lizie had been busy preparing the cottage for her grand childrens' arrivals and had a good idea when they would arrive thanks to the cell phone movement! Now let me see she thought, the girls can take the back bedroom which is a little smaller than the other one at the front of the cottage where the boys would sleep. Both rooms had wonderful views of the sea and Gundaga Island. Today the sea looked an especially sparkly shade of blue, very calm and quite inviting, umm she thought, maybe we can swim later and be totally lazy on the beach. Ah the long hazy lazy days of summer being just around the corner oh yes!

Several blasts of car horns brought Lizie running out of the cottage to greet everyone. Amazingly they had all somehow managed to arrive at the same time.

"Hello" said Lizie as the cars pulled up. "Good trip I take it?"

The kids all piled out of their seats and made a dash for Lizie who by now had braced herself in readiness!

"Oh it's so good to see you all, my how you have all grown in height."

The younger ones squealed with delight whilst the older ones gave out hugs and the girls kisses too.

"Come, let's go inside, bring your things in too, cool lemonade all round."

"Yes please and any chocolate chip cookies to go with that too?" asked Catrin.

"Never a moment without them" said Lizie as she prepared the snacks and drinks.

When everyone had had their fill of cookies and lemonade the older ones decided to un-pack their things in the designated rooms. It was pretty easy to see just where they were all to sleep.

"That's what I like said Christian, sleeping bags and no fussing with bed sheets!" giving Sam a friendly punch in the arm as he said it.

"Sure suits me too" said Sam as he prepared to take a run and dive into the soft mattress of his bed. "Yeehah!"

The girls on the other hand were much quieter than the boys at settling in.

"I love this room" exclaimed Abbey.

Even though it was a much smaller room than the boys' bed room it had lots of windows, some on the side of the cottage too giving out great views of the sea and Gundaga Island.

"I hope that we get lots of thunder storms whilst we are here, the whole sea will light up" mused Maddie dreamily and continued to put her things away in an orderly fashion.

Catrin hadn't said much but had worked quietly sorting out where everything was to go, last but not least her rag doll with the yellow stringy hair placing her on her pillow with the feet just inside the sleeping bag.

"There Maggedy Catrin said, that's where we will sleep tonight all cosy and warm."

By now it was getting time for the moms and dads to leave for home. Babe the whole time had been sniffing around the garden (yard) looking for squirrels, rabbits and anything else he could scent.

"Hey kids shouted Lizie her voice traveling up the stairs like a gale force blast, time to say bye for two weeks."

The clatter of many feet sounded like a stampede of elephants coming down the stairs as they all made their way outside to bid farewell to their parents.

"See you in two weeks."

*   *   *

CHAPTER TWO

THE SMELL OF FRESH BAKED biscuits filled the air making everyone hungry for breakfast. "Come and get it whilst it's hot" bellowed Lizie.

Little curls peeked out from underneath the sleeping bag and at first Kenzie wondered just where she was. Then she heard the waves breaking gently on the beach from the open window. "I think I will need my bucket and spade again today" she said in her quietest voice and began to suck her thumb.

After breakfast it took about five minutes to walk down to the beach, the morning sun feeling quite warm, brilliant light cascading down on everyones' shoulders. The sea shimmered and looked very inviting for a swim again.

"Let's make a camp over here" yelled Christian at the others.

"Well we have the whole beach to ourselves at the moment so anywhere will do" Lizie jestered and prepared to make herself comfortable in her beach chair. Caleb and Sam decided to explore a little whilst Christian and Cole set about building the makeshift camp with the beach chairs and towels. As expected the younger two immediately began to dig in the soft sand with their little red spades which would keep them busy, well for now! The girls decided to sit at the waters' edge, the waves rippling over their toes making them squeal with sheer delight.

"Ooh, that feels a bit cold" Catrin said, then all three of them engaged in girl chatter which was of no surprise.

Sam and Caleb had continued to walk the beach often looking out to sea and Gundaga Island wondering what it would be like to go out there. A day trip would be fantastic but first they would have to find an old row boat that someone had no use for.

"I bet Lizie knows of someone Sam said, let's ask her when we get back."

"Good idea" added Caleb.

As they continued on both boys noticed a glinting flash of light coming from the island at various intervals. Probably day trippers they thought who would be out there for the day with binoculars as many species of birds inhabited the trees.

"Lizie, do you know of anyone with an old row boat that they would want to get rid of?"

"As a matter of fact I do" she replied, "Old Mr. Barnabus Winkle has a couple of them which haven't seen water for some time now." "He lives just two sand dunes down from me so I can arrange for you all to meet him maybe this afternoon, but if not then tomorrow OK."

The afternoon was quite hot so they all stayed on the beach swimming, a couple of games of soccer and refuge in the shade that the makeshift camp gave. Lizie had packed a picnic with all sorts of goodies and lots of water to quench their thirsts.

She made a phone call whilst on the beach to Mr. Winkle. "Hello there" she shouted down the phone, "is that Mr. Winkle, and how are you today?" From the response he was doing very well so Lizie continued to explain about her grand childrens' two week visit making arrangements for them all to meet in the morning at around ten o'clock.

Bedtime soon came around and to be honest all were more than ready to call it a day.

"Must be all the fresh air and keeping busy" Cole said as he snuggled down in his sleeping bag relishing the freshness of it umm.

"I wonder what Mr. Winkle is like" Christians' muffled voice from half way into his sleeping bag sleepily said but there was no response from the others as they were all fast asleep!

Kenzie was sleeping with her Santa doll clutched tightly to her little chest whilst the other three girls lay awake going over the wonderful day that they had had.

"I wish that I could live here all the time" said Maddie.

"Me too me too" came Abbeys' reply.

"I love it here too" said Catrin as she settled down with Maggedy in her sleeping bag and with that slowly went to sleep.

The children woke up with a start BANG BANG BANG! What in the world was that awful noise coming from downstairs? and with that they all rushed down to where the commotion was coming from.

"I thought that would get your attention and to announce that breakfast is ready" Lizie said laughing. Dippy eggs, toast, cereal, juice and milk, what ever they wanted. Lizie hadn't told them about the gong that she had bought so it was quite a surprise to all of them.

"HA! we'll get used to it" drooled Christian as egg yolk dripped from his chin making the others laugh too.

Walking to Mr. Winkles' place was refreshing for them and no sooner entered his driveway when two row boats, one propped up against a fence, the other lying in the tall grass came into view.

"Wow, look at those" Sam excitedly burst out.

"What if they have holes in them?" his sister said.

"Well if they do we can fix the problem" Christian said in answer to his cousins' question.

"Good morning Lizie, lovely as always to see you and my what alot of grandchildren you have" said Mr. Winkle.

"Oh there are two more, twins infact at home with their mother, James and Jarid" announced Lizie and began to laugh yet again.

"Well mi little 'uns tis very nice to meet you all" he said and began the task of trying to remember all their names. "It would be easier to give you all a number, aye I could do that" and chuckled at his own humor!

Camden was mesmorised with Mr. Winkles' eyes as one of them didn't move when the other one did. I wonder if that is what happens to some grown ups eyes he thought, but Lizies' eyes were OK. Mr. Winkle could see the curious look in Camdens' stare and decided to tell him about his glass eye.

"When I was a boy mi little 'un another boy threw a stone at me which hit me squarely in the eye, the doctors couldn't save it so a glass eye was the remedy."

"Does it ever come out?" asked Caleb.

"Sometimes I take it out if mi socket is irritated, but believe you me it looks far better with it in."

"Mr. Winkle, the children were wondering if you would be interested in giving them one of the old row boats that they could potter around in?" asked Lizie.

"Well now, let's see said the elderly man, I take it that the smaller 'uns would be with you Lizie, so that means a boat big enough to take seven little 'uns." "I do have an extra long row boat in mi shed which would do just fine for 'um" and continued to stroke his captains' beard.

The boat needed painting badly but thankfully it didn't have any holes in it at all. A good few blows with a hammer would fix the seats and the oar locks some nice brass screws to hold them securely.

"We can do all that, said the four boys all at once, we would love the challenge Mr. Winkle."

"Well we girls can help out too" announced Maddie in a haughty tone not wanting to be outsmarted by boys!

So with that they had themselves a row boat thanks to Barnabus Winkle. It didn't take too much energy to carry the boat back to Lizies' place complete with the oars which needed painting as well.

In the shed at the back of the cottage there were some old cans of paint left over from the cottage renovations which would do the job nicely. Yellow, lime green and teal were the colors of choice. With much deliberation between them all it was decided to paint one half of the boat yellow and the other half lime green with teal colored oars. But first the wood would have to be sanded down and primed in readiness for the paint. The electric sander made light work of it, Christian, Caleb, Cole and Sam taking it in turns with it. Meanwhile the girls had been sorting out the paints and brushes for when needed. The seats were a bit warped but with a little patience were soon in place.

"This is great, I love to hammer wood into place with nails" Sam said.

"Well just watch your fingers there Sam Caleb cautioned, no accidents please he added."

Lizie had taken Camden and Kenzie down to the beach again to dig around. She noticed that Gundaga Island seemed busy today with periods of flashing lights but thought no more of it.

As the afternoon wore on the row boat started to have a little less of that abandoned look, still had much more work to be done on it but would be ready for the water probably in two days. The starboard side was painted yellow and the port side lime green with teal oars and black bands around where they would fit into the oar locks. Needless to say that for the next two days they were absolutely covered in paint but Lizie thought that it was wonderful that they were all working so hard on the boat in readiness for it's launch in two days. Mr. Winkle had promised that he would check everything out before rowing out to Gundaga Island began.

Two days later the boat was ready for it's launch into the water so everyone decided an early night was key. Mr. Winkle was coming over at around eight o'clock in the morning to check everything out for safety.

On the late night news that night an important bulletin was announced that a bank had been robbed that morning in the next town to Gundaga, a town called Port Camjas only five miles due east. The thieves getting away with an un-disclosed amount of money and possibly some jewels or gold bars too. Be on the look out for a dark brown work van, four suspects possibly five is the message from the police.

Wow thought Lizie, just wait until the kids hear about this and with that she also called it a night.

*   *   *

CHAPTER THREE

RAP-A-RAP-A-RAP-RAP WENT THE SOUND OF knuckles on the cottage door.

That has to be Mr. Winkle thought Lizie and right on time too eight o'clock. The children had been up since six o'clock so they were more than ready for Mr. Winkles' arrival.

"Good morning Mr. Winkle greeted Lizie, they have been up for quite some time now and are ready when you are to test out the boat.

"Aye Lizie, an' a good mornin' tu you too mi dear, and how are mi little 'uns this bright and sunny day?" he asked.

"Very well" replied Cole grinning from ear to ear.

OK then, let's get down to the beach and see just what this row boat will do for us" said Mr. Winkle.

"Well 'eavens tu be mi little 'uns" an astonished Mr. Winkle let out. "You sure 'ave been busy these last few days, and my what bright colors you all picked out." "D'ya have a name for the boat? As tis bad luck not to before she goes into the water."

"We never thought of that chimed the kids, do you have any ideas or suggestions for us?.

"I think it's up to you little 'uns to name your own boat for extra good luck" he said.

"What about Plain Sailing" suggested Sam.

"Or Easy Going" shouted Caleb.

"I know a good one, Rainbow" said Abbey.

"It cannot be Rainbow as there isn't any pink on it" scoffed Christian.

"Well there will be when I get on board wearing my favorite pink shorts!" smirked Catrin.

The kids all fell about laughing at that remark, even Mr. Winkle ho-ho and hummed at that too. After some time the word adventure came up which seemed to sum up what their vacation was going to be all about. So it was then decided to name the boat Adventure which would be painted on both sides later.

As the boat edged it's way towards the water it made snake like lines in the soft golden sand. Whoosh went a wave as it slapped alongside the boat lifting it up momentarily clearly wetting everyones' shorts as they clung to the sides. Christian being the eldest one at thirteen was given the job of testing out the oars in the re-vamped oar locks, making sure that there were no sudden leaks anywhere. Complete with a life jacket on he manovered the boat so that the bow now faced the open sea and began to row with all his might.

Aye thought Mr. Winkle, the boy sure can row a boat and felt confident that they would be safe. Next up was Sam to have a go then Caleb followed by Cole all proving strong enough to take over for a bit lest Christian became tired. For the rest of the day they stayed close to the shore taking turns with the rowing as tomorrow they were going out to Gundaga Island for the day which would be so much fun. The girls had the job of painting "Adventure" on both sides of the boat in neat black letters once the boys had finished up rowing practise.

"Keep it neat girls" said Christian.

"Aye aye Captain, we will."

After a long day on the beach and not much lunch they were all ravenous for supper. Lizie had had the hindsight to make a large lasagna with garlic bread which smelt oh so yummy. Camden and Kenzie had spent the day at the cottage playing in the garden making a change from digging down on the beach.

"I noticed a bit of a swell this morning, the waves being larger than usual, probably a storm is in the forecast."

"Lizie I would love to see a storm" said Maddie.

"Me too added Abbey, I would curl up in my sleeping bag and hide in between the flashes of lightening."

"Well we boys are not afraid of a silly thunder storm" Caleb said.

"I might be" muttered Camden.

"Oh you'll be fine with us" Christian chuckled and felt a protectiveness towards his small brother.

Sure enough the weather forecast was predicting thunder storms for later on that night.

"I just hope that it will not spoil your plans to visit Gundaga Island tomorrow, we'll just have to see" Lizie exclaimed.

Because things had been so busy Lizie had forgotten to mention the bank robbery that had taken place yesterday and with further thought decided that it could wait till morning. Besides the robbery wasn't going to affect their lives, and in any case the men responsible would be far gone by now, miles away infact.

Once again it was bedtime for all, Kenzie being younger than the rest had gone earlier and was deep in dream land.

"Can we read for a while?" asked Sam.

"Sure you can if the light doesn't bother the others" Lizie replied.

"I have a night light so that I can read under the covers if need be Lizie."

"OK sweetheart" she said and with that went to check up on the girls. They were in the throws of cleaning their teeth and asked through their white frothy mouths if they too could read for a while. But instead of reading they had decided to whisper to one another making plans for their first trip out to Gundaga Island. They were so excited that they couldn't sleep but then out of the night sky came the distant rumble of thunder.

"Ohh, I think the storm is on it's way" shrieked Catrin and dive bombed well inside her sleeping bag with Maggedy her precious rag doll. The girls were all similar in age, Catrin was now eight, Abbey nine and Maddie ten who were more than happy to be together and so close as cousins could be, what good friends too! That could be said for the boys also, infact Maddie and Cole were born on the same day Maddie being forty minutes older than Cole so a special bond kind of existed between them. All in all they all got along with one another and with only the odd spat.

A rumble of thunder echoed through the night sky again getting closer as storms do, like a menacing wolf on the prowl. Soon there would be lightening too to cast it's brilliance around, unleashing the secrets of the dark corners of the night.

One by one everyone went to sleep but not for long as all of a sudden there was an almighty bang bringing the once sleeping children from their pleasant dreams to the harsh reality of the storm which seemed to be right over head. The rain lashed down in torrents as the wind blew violently which made the trees moan and creak. Another enormous flash of blue lightening penetrated the cottage followed by yet another boom of thunder. Kenzie was sitting up in her sleeping bag sucking her thumb almost on the brink of tears as Lizie ran up the stairs to comfort her and anyone else who was scared too.

They all huddled together in the girls' room occasionally looking out to sea. Another blue pink flash crackled out of the sky followed by yet another mighty bang which shook the whole cottage. Christian was looking out to sea and Gundaga Island when he thought though through the bad visibility that the storm was creating there seemed to be a light of some sort moving about on the island. Who could possibly be out there and in this storm he pondered, no I must be mistaken.

"Hey you guys, come and look through the window as I think that I see a light out on Gundaga Island." All but Kenzie and Camden went to stare out of the window looking out over the angry looking sea, focusing on the island.

"Christian you are right" they all agreed, there was a light moving out there and whoever it was must be wet through by now.

"Maybe some day trippers who were obviously not tuned into the weather forecast and became stranded, still there are many caves to take shelter in from the storm" Lizie told them.

The sea was extremely rough pounding on the beach below.

"Good thing that we tied Adventure up good with the ropes that Mr. Winkle gave to us as she would have been blown away by now."

"Yeah, and storing her up-side down was a good idea too then we won't have to bail her out in the morning" said the boys between themselves.

The storm continued for about another hour or so but becoming weaker with each passing moment, the flashes of lightening coming at various intervals but not followed by the banging booms as it had been doing.

"It makes a pretty picture out there with the lightening" Maddie said, "just as I thought it would do and I got my wish too."

"How come you boys ended up in the girls room with us as I thought that thunder storms were silly and nothing to be afraid of?" asked Lizie.

Flushing up a little knowing full well that they had been caught out Caleb decided to get them out of a tight spot.

"We thought that you girls would be scared and so we came in to protect you all, I do hope that we did help you."

Lizie began to smile to herself and decided not to take the matter any further even though she knew that the boys had been scared she just thanked them in the best way she could.

*   *   *

CHAPTER FOUR

THREE BACK PACKS, SEVEN TOWELS, plus seven life jackets were placed at the side door of the cottage in readiness to take down to the beach where the boat was. The storm of last night had cooled the air and with a mild breeze it would make for a perfect day to explore Gundaga Island. The sun shone brightly in the morning sky making the droplets of rain on the grass sparkle like diamonds.

"Who is up first for rowing the boat?" asked Cole curiously.

"Not me" said Caleb.

"Nor me" said Sam.

Lizie hearing this came up with the idea that the oldest should be the first, then followed by the second oldest which would be Sam, then Caleb and lastly Cole. This proved to be a fair settlement between the boys and so it was the perfect solution.

Once again it had been busy in the kitchen with the usual breakfast fare though Kenzie had requested a "dwam swamdwidge" translating to a jelly sandwich in American. Lizie being originally from England referred to it as a jam butty and so every once in a while she would come out with the British version of things. She loved to test the kids to see if they could remember the differences and only the other day she did just that. For lunch she had asked them all who would like 'Welsh Rarebit' which is just cheese on toast. Camden upon hearing this had said no to that kind of lunch because he didn't want to eat 'Welsh Rabbits' until he realised just what it was!

The baggage was picked up as they all left the cottage, packs swung over shoulders, towels strung over arms with life jackets around torsos. Lizie was going into town with the younger two and gave the adventurous seven a good farewell for the day with repeated warnings of please be careful.

Reception for the cell phones was not always good to non existent so as a back up system Lizie had arranged with them that at noon they send flashes of light by means of a mirror across the water to Gundaga Point where Lizies' cottage stood. There she would be able to see this through her binoculars, then to be repeated every two hours as she would be down on the beach as usual.

Their boat Adventure moved easily down to the water after righting her up and placing all their stuff in the bow. Space was limited so it was just as well that they had only the three back packs etc. One thing they all noticed that there were lots of footprints in the sand some of them leading up to some rocks further up the beach.

"Well maybe because it's a cooler morning, I mean it's so much fresher after the storm" said Maddie. They all seemed to agree with her.

"Ahoy there mi little shipmates" bellowed a voice from far aloft. It was Mr. Winkle waving at them from the cliffs above the beach. He had come to wish them a safe voyage to the island and with fair weather in the forecast they were sure of a great day. He had previously given them instructions to row straight across the water and to head for a rocky point in the middle of Gundagas' cove. Crossing the small area of water from the mainland wouldn't be a problem either as there were no dangerous rocks hidden from view beneath the aqua blue waters.

"We had better get going" said Christian as they had promised Lizie to be back for no later than six o'clock.

Adventure bobbed over the gentle waves as one by one they all climbed in. Caleb was the last one aboard as he had been making sure that the boat kept clear of the sandy bottom with the extra weight that had been added.

"Haul up the anchor" said Christian laughing (there was no anchor!) and with that he heaved back on the oars Adventure slowly leaving the shore. Mr. Winkle grew smaller up on the cliff top, he was still waving with all his might!

"Oh this is so exciting" exclaimed Abbey, "I feel as though we are going on a pirate adventure."

"What were those songs that sailors used to sing?" asked Sam.

"I think I remember Lizie telling me about sea-shanties" Maddie added.

"Yeah, didn't the sailors sing them as they rowed their tall ships" Caleb suggested.

"Think so, and then there is that one toddler song about row row row your boat" Cole proffered.

Row row row your boat
Gently o'er the sea
Merrily merrily merrilee
Life is but a dream.

They all kept on singing as Gundaga Island came nearer looking so much more different than what it did from the mainland. Still rowing strongly Christian showed no signs of fatigue, the excitement probably staving it off. Adventure had proved to be a good boat as she shimmied up the beach, finally they were on Gundaga Island.

Lizies' trip into town with Kenzie and Camden turned out to be much fun. After sorting out the registration for the boat with Mr. Winkle she took the little ones down to the wharf where many fishing boats were moored. All kinds of colors met their eyes, reds, blues, yellows and whites. Yards and yards of netting folded around the boats put to good use when trawling for fish out in the vast open sea.

The fishermen were all busy with their morning catches of fish, gutting and cleaning, storing on ice ready for the market. Then the boats had to be hosed down and made ready for the next morning to dawn when they would all head out to sea again in the hopes of yet another good catch. Their yellow plastic suits were awash with water and fish guts, the air having that salty fish smell which was attracting the many squalking gulls that hovered overhead. Waiting for their next meal be it edible or not would swoop down at intervals to get what they could causing fights between them. What a frenzy!

Lizie also explained to the two children that the rubber tires on the sides of the boats stopped them from repeatedly banging against the side of the stone pier. The thick slime green ropes kept the boats firmly at their moorings.

Gundaga was a smallish town but boasted many colorful houses some three storeys high, the usual gift shops which always reside at coastal places and some eating places too which Lizie thought might be a good idea for supper tonight.

Port Camjas on the other hand was a much larger town than Gundaga and had to offer anything for the locals and tourists alike. It housed a bigger fishing port and with many hotels/motels for the annual vacationers. Mr. Winkle was born in Port Camjas, spending all his boy hood there, the passion for boats always with him, hence he was a fisher man all his adult life. Generations of his family before him had also been men of the sea, it ran through their veins. His wife of many years had sadly passed away two years ago and unfortunately were not blessed with children. He was now three score and ten which put him at age seventy. He was proving to be a good friend to Lizie and was kind of taking her nine grandchildren under his wing, especially the seven out on the island right now.

*   *   *

CHAPTER FIVE

M ANY WILLING HANDS PULLED ADVENTURE up the beach free from
the waves that caressed the shoreline of the island.

"There that should hold" said Christian as he tied one rope off
around a thick stake of wood embedded in the sand. Now the decision
was what to do next.

"Shall we explore some of these caves first?" asked Maddie.

"Good thinking cousin" replied Sam as he had been thinking exactly
the same thing. The first cave was not too dark, small though and because
a boulder of rock jutted out they couldn't go too far inside.

"One down many more to go into yet" said Caleb and with that they
continued on to the next one which turned out to be very similar to the
one they had just come out of.

"I hope these caves are not all the same" a slightly disappointed
Abbey added.

Sure enough the third cave gave them all hope as it turned out to
be larger and therefore they could all walk further back into it, the light
from outside becoming dimmer.

"Hey, who has the flashlight?" asked Christian.

Un-zipping one of the back packs Sam said "I do, here you are."

"Eeew! exclaimed Catrin, it is gross in here, it drips and is smelly."

"It's because of the lack of light and fresh air that the sea weed never
dries out which makes that pong, there are more than likely bats living in
here too, bat poop yuk!" Caleb had to add.

With the thought of bats the girls began to squeal which echoed
throughout the cave. Listen to that they all thought then Sam began to
shout.

"Sam, Sam, Sam" until the echo grew quieter. Then in turn they all
had a go at shouting their names one echo over another which was quite
deafning.

"We need to get out of here" shouted Cole which added to the
wailing sound and with that they all turned and ran at top speed out of
the cave until once again into the welcoming sunshine.

"No more caves for me, that was just too scary" Catrin shrieked.

"Oh you'll be fine Catrin, we still have more to go into" then Sam put a re-assuring arm about her shoulders.

"I do hope you are right Sam" and felt quite a protectiveness from her cousin.

Noon was approaching and remembering that they needed to relay a message to Lizie to signal that all was OK with them. Maddie reached in one of the back packs for her mirror and asked "who knows how to do this?"

"Here let me" and with that Christian began to point the mirror at an angle with the sun and Gundaga Point where Lizies' cottage looked like a small black dot.

"There that should do it, she will have seen that signal from us."

Lizie back on the mainland had seen the signal through the binoculars and felt very happy that all was well with them out there.

"Right you two, are you both ready for the beach?" she asked.

Think so as their little red spades and pails were clutched tightly in their hands, towels strung around their necks. The picnic basket had all sorts of things in it so there would be no reason to go back to the cottage for the whole afternoon.

Out on the island the adventurous seven had decided to have lunch first before climbing the cliffs to explore amongst the trees and tall grasses. Food was plentiful, peanut butter and jelly, salami or ham sandwiches, cheese cubes, granola bars, fruit, apple juice boxes and water.

After eating and drinking their fill everything was packed up and stored with the ice blocks behind some rocks in the shade. Taking a bottle of water each they began the steep climb up the cliff by way of an old worn gravel path which curved in and out of the tall grasses and on up to where the trees began. The twitter of many birds met their ears and in between the thick foliage a flash of color would swoop by.

"I knew that I should have brought my bird spotting book with me" exclaimed Caleb.

"And a pair of binoculars too would have been handy" Sam said.

The island was home to Oak, Weeping Willows, Elm, Maple and Pine trees, with hawthorn, blackberry and raspberry bushes too.

After a while when they were done bird watching and recognising the various trees Cole mentioned that it would be about time to make their way back to the beach to send Lizie another re-assuring message that all was well with them.

"Yes, you are right Cole as we did promise Lizie faithfully that we would relay flashes to her" said Christian and Abbey almost together making them laugh. Maddie fumbled inside the back pack once again to find the mirror which she handed over to Christian. He tweeked it at the sun and direction of Gundaga Beach where Lizie would be by now with Camden and Kenzie.

"Ah very good" muttered Lizie to herself as she watched the flashes of light shimmer across to her, all is well over there.

"Camden, let's dig over there by those rocks" Kenzie said and began to run as fast as her little legs would go, Camden in hot persuit waving his spade in the air. It was a lovely warm not too hot afternoon as Lizie settled down to read some of her book, one about shipwrecks!

Clunk, thump was the noise that their spades made as they hit something down in the sand.

"What is it?" asked Kenzie.

"I don't know" but continued to dig whilst Kenzie wondered off a little to make another hole in the sand. Slowly a metal box appeared out of the hole and after some fiddling he managed to open it. There was a scroll of paper inside and once un-folded all that could be seen was a mass of letters on it which didn't make any sense to the pair of them.

"Let's go and show this to Lizie Kenzie" and she nodded in agreement.

"Lizie, look what we have found in the sand" they both squealed, "it has some letters on it." Lizie took hold of the scroll and looked at the message written on it, but wait a minute this doesn't make any sense to me either as it's written backwards. Without a mirror to make it out she decided to leave it until later, wondering just who "Smudgy" was!

Back on the island the seven had kept themselves busy with swimming, eating the rest of the lunch and mouth watering fruit.

"Who is up for going into another cave before we leave?" asked Sam.

The girls were a definite no to his suggestion and thought that maybe it was just for the boys this time. So off they went to explore the fourth

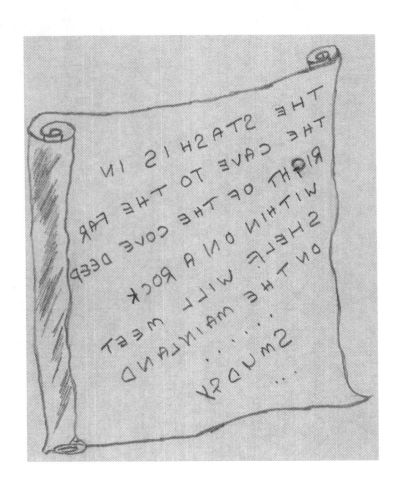

Smudgys' scrolled message.

cave which was not really interesting, yes it was dark and smelly as the other ones were. Thank heaven for flash lights then suddenly something swooped down past their heads.

"What was that?" Caleb asked startled as they all were.

"It's a bat" yelled Christian, "did you see it's red eyes, I'm outta here!" and with that they all turned heel to run but not before another bat came straight for them at full speed brushing the tops of their heads!

"Arrgh" they all shouted, "they are trying to peck at our heads, run."

And run they did at top speed back into the warm sunshine leaving the bats and the noisy echoes behind.

"Whatever is the matter?" asked the girls. "You all look as if you have just seen a ghost" they continued.

"Bats, two of them came skimming at us trying to peck our heads" Cole panted as he tried to catch his breath.

"Blood red eyes that looked right at you as if to say just what are you doing in our cave!" garbled Sam quickly.

"Wish it had been a ghost rather than those nasty bats" a terrified Caleb added.

"Good thing you girls didn't come with us, you would have been frozen to the spot with fear" Cole said his breathing getting back to normal.

"Yeah it was a bit much and there is still one more cave that we haven't been into yet" gasped Christian.

"Well that last cave can stay un-explored by us anyway" said Maddie quite meaningfully.

"Totally agree" came from Catrin.

Checking on the time it was almost five o'clock which meant that it was time to pack up and start the trip back to Gundaga. There Lizie would be waiting for them. Adventure was soon bobbing on the waves and apart from Sam whose turn it was to make sure that the boat kept clear of the sandy sea bed. With everyone on board again Christian once again heaved back with the oars, Adventure cutting through the water with ease.

Through the binoculars Lizie could see the boat getting closer with all seven in it thank goodness. Bet their day has been one of the best she thought to herself. "Hey Kenzie, Camden, they are on their way back."

Excited the two of them happily began to jump up and down, what a lovely night they were all going to have.

*   *   *

CHAPTER SIX

S UPPER AT THE RESTAURANT WAS quite eventful with everyone chattering all at once about their day, then the story of the bat invasion came up in the conversation.

"BATS!" Lizie said at the top of her voice, "you could have been badly hurt by those vicious things, little vampires they are." "That's it zero caves on your next visit over there." Sam re-assured Lizie that going into another cave was not an option, that it would have to be an extreme reason to do so which was not going to happen. The rest were in total agreement.

The walk back to the cottage was a pleasant one, passing Mr. Winkles' place was all quiet with him no where to be seen.

"By the way Lizie said as they got back home Kenzie and Camden found this on the beach whilst digging by the rocks." "Looks to be some kind of message written by someone called Smudgy, it looks kind of loopy as it's written backwards!" Probably some kind of joke she thought to herself then told the children so.

"Let's take it up-stairs suggested Maddie, I have a mirror in my bag remember." Once up-stairs they all sat in a ring cross legged on the floor. Caleb held up the scroll with the message whilst Maddie held up the mirror towards it.

"This is serious" yelled Christian, "stolen money hidden in one of the caves on Gundaga Island, the one cave that we didn't go into!"

"Is that what the stash means?" asked Catrin.

"Yep" Christian said to his sister.

"Well we will just have to go back and soon" she replied. All were for that!

"But what about Lizie?, she will not let us go back if she knew about the stolen money on the island, better still, where are the thieves?" asked Cole.

"I get it, that's why there were lots of footprints by the rocks this morning, it must have been that Smudgy guy and his mate putting the box in the sand" added Maddie.

"And thanks to Camden and Kenzie finding it we will now be able to help capture the crooks and bring the money back" an excited Sam said.

"You make it sound so easy but it won't be quite that easy" Christian had to say.

"We can only do our best keeping ourselves safe too" commented Abbey.

"Lizie would you mind if we went out to Gundaga Island again tomorrow?" asked Christian.

"Well providing that the weather forecast is good then I don't see why not, and as long as messages are sent back to me that all is OK with you all then I don't mind at all."

"Oh good, I'll go and tell the others, they will be so excited."

"By the way Christian, there was a bank robbery the other day in Port Camjas, money, maybe jewels and or gold bars, but I expect that the thieves are long gone by now."

Christian was bursting to tell the others up-stairs and went up the steps two at a time!

"Hey guess what, Lizie has just told me about a bank robbery that took place a few days ago in Port Camjas, money, could be jewels and gold bars too!" All eyes were on Christian as big and as round as eyes could get.

"That does it, we are definitely going back tomorrow" said Maddie.

"No kiddin', did you ask Lizie if that was OK, she doesn't mind?" Caleb asked.

"Providing that the weather is fine and that we relay messages back then Lizie didn't see why not."

"Hopefully we can stay one day ahead of the thieves seeing that they won't get their message off the beach, then it will take more time for them to contact the others in their gang." "By then we will have it all to turn in to the cops and maybe be small town heros too" Christian said smilingly. They all liked the sound of that but not one word to Lizie which all agreed on. The younger two hadn't really been paying too much attention playing amongst themselves.

"Lizie, can we please pack a picnic between us to take tomorrow? we can make it up" suggested Abbey.

"Of course you can luvvy" and hugged Abbey like there was no tomorrow, but there was going to be a tomorrow, one of the best!

*   *   *

CHAPTER SEVEN

APART FROM THE YOUNGER TWO sleep was hard to come by knowing the heroic efforts that they would have to endure the following day. Each of them in their bedrooms whispered to one another, would they be famous or not?, would they be harmed if the thieves found them out? Stomach butterflies were abound, churning which made their hearts beat a little faster! At around three in the morning a low rumble of thunder growled in the distance waking up Christian and Sam.

"Oh no, let's hope that it will be a quick storm going through" sighed Sam.

"I think so, but if not, should it mess up our plans for tomorrow then just think that if we are messed up then so will the thieves."

"Christian you are so smart, you think of everything" and with that they both lay awake to listen for the next rumble to happen which it did. The lightening began followed by crackles of thunder but nowhere as severe as it had been the other night when it had really boomed. The sea became rougher but in a way it sounded soothing to them and it wasn't about to etch it's mark in the sand too much. The two boys fell asleep again only to be wakened by a horrific BANG BANG BANG. No it wasn't thunder, it was Lizies' gong announcing that breakfast was ready again.

"I thought that you said that we would get used to that awful noise Christian" a yawning quartet of boys said sleepily.

"Well Lizie hasn't used it since that first time so it's bound to be a surprise, kind of like a wake up call would you say."

"Nice wake up call" a grumpy Caleb said.

"Remember we have alot to do today and not a word to Lizie" Christian stressed to them and began to get dressed in his usual denim shorts and tee shirt.

"I know that I said we would not go into the caves again and that it would have to be very important to do so thinking that it would never happen. But it is very important so in a way we are not telling Lizie lies as that would be the last thing I would want to do" Sam said.

"Tricky as it is Sam, but remember we are trying to do some good here and have an adventure too" as Christian put up a friendly high five for his cousin to match!

Breakfast was yet again a yummy affair with lots of goodies to eat, the list was endless as they all tucked in. The gong had just stopped making it's clanging noise when little Kenzie who was in the throws of sucking her thumb and trailing her blanky to the breakfast table decided not to look for a second where she was going. Low and behold she collided with the gong setting off that ear piercing racket again she almost leaping out of her pj's! The others were hysterical laughing making toast crumbs fly out over the table from their mouths. Poor Sam who had just been taking a mouthful of orange juice sprayed the table and now his face dripped with the liquid! Oh boy what an absolutely hilarious moment thought Lizie.

"Kenzie sweetheart, are you alright?" a concerned Lizie asked her small grand daughter. Kenzie was not amused and began to sulk at everyone for laughing but not for long and it was then that her bottom lip went back to normal!

"Now let's see, we mustn't forget the binoculars" muttered Christian to himself. The picnic basket was ready and waiting for them all to grab.

"Are we all ready?" asked Caleb.

Lizie bade them all a farewell for the day at the door of the cottage with the usual cautions and stick together.

"Thank you Lizie" they all chorused and made their way down to the beach where more than one adventure waited for them! The boat was fairly dry as not too much rain had fallen during the night. Within moments the boat was in the water, belongings stored in the bow again. Cole had made sure that the boat stayed clear of the sandy bottom then everyone was on board and ready for off. Gundaga Island here we come but for a very different reason this time!

Anticipation was running through all seven minds, what if the thieves are armed and dangerous waiting for us. What if they have already been and taken the stolen goods, or what if they have set traps for us. One thing for sure is that they wouldn't know until they were on the island, and worse still approaching that cave!

Christian rowed strongly easy to see that he really enjoyed it. Adventure made a whooshing sound as she cut through the calm water, the gulls making habitual calls to one another as they winged it through the salty air.

Adventure was tied up closer to the water than usual should they need a quicker get-a-way, keeping all their belongings in the bow.

"Just get stuff out when we need it" suggested Christian.

"Aye aye capt'n!" joked Caleb and Sam together.

It seemed a bit strange to them knowing their reason for returning and so soon, not to mention the courage needed to enter the fifth cave which was the farthest one out to the right of the cove.

"There may be bats again that might attack us, but just think of finding all that stolen money . . . . and hoping that we can get it all into our boat" said Caleb.

The boat was also close to the cave so that there wouldn't be too great a distance to drag the sacks or whatever the stash was in over to it. Good thinking prevailed all round!

"OK, here goes, into the cave we disappear, be brave all of you" Sam stressed.

"We will, we have to over come our fears" said Catrin.

Without further thought they all went into the cave, into the abyss, that great black entrance to which the future held, What would become of them?, and just what would they find?

*   *   *

CHAPTER EIGHT

A BROWN WORK VAN PULLED INTO the town of Gundaga, "Here at last" said the gruff man who went by the name of Nick Sharpe, his nick name being Razor. "I sure hope that Smudgy put the message where he said he would for us down on Gundaga Beach."

"Well he said by a certain rock, so let's go and see" said his mate who was known as Planks, his real name being Woody Splinter. The third man who was with them was known as Will Sting, his nick name being Nettles joined in the conversation about Smudgy not being reliable. Smudgy was teamed up with a guy called Neil Chappell alias Pews who was kind of the nerd of the five of them.

The three men made their way down to the beach and out to the intended rock. Much to their surprise a large hole was staring back at them!

"Looks as though someone has already been here and dug up the box which contained the message from Smudgy telling us where the money is hidden" growled Nettles.

"Now what are we supposed to do?" asked Planks feeling total bewilderment too.

"Just how are we supposed to find our stash now?, that Smudgy, I knew that we should have stayed together from first robbing the bank, hissed Razor, but staying together wouldn't have worked as well, splitting up as we did should help us to stay un-detected."

"It seemed like a good idea at the time" added Nettles.

"It just ain't right" Planks muttered.

Scouring the beach for further clues their wishes were granted as they came across many footsteps in the sand. Obviously a boat had been dragged down the beach to the waters' edge. The grooves bearing witness as well that some people had taken a boat out probably to Gundaga Island, and some of those footprints looked to be childrens!

"Hey Planks, Nettles hollered Razor, d'ya suppose that some kids dug up the message, figured it all out and are now looking for what belongs to us"

His face began to twitch after he had said all this.

Smudgy said he would take it all to a remote place he thought and that there island would make the perfect spot.

"No one lives on that island" he said aloud.

"How d'ya know that?" asked Nettles.

"Just listening to the folks around here since we arrived" replied Planks.

Barnabus Winkle had decided to take a walk along the beach after letting his breakfast settle in his ever growing stomach. Umm he thought to himself I am not getting any smaller by any means, but at least I am happy enough inspite of not being on the sea anymore and living on my own.

It was a very pleasant morning, the sun shining down, it's yellow matching that of a huge egg yolk. Mr. Winkle took his time making it down to the beach where-upon he came across three rather scruffy looking men who seemed a bit un-sure of themselves.

"Mornin' hailed Mr. Winkle, can I help you with anything?, are you new in town as I don't recollect seeing you all before."

"Mornin' to you too, sorry I didn't catch your name" said Razor.

"Winkle, Barnabus Winkle, an' old sea dog and local."

"Well nice to see you Mr. Winkle replied Razor, my name is Nick Sharpe and here we have Woody Splinter and Will Sting mi mates."

"That there island, I hear that just birds nest over there, do many people visit to bird watch?" asked Razor to Mr. Winkle.

"Aye that's Gundaga Island alright, nope no people live over there just gets bird spotters." "It would be a good place to hide something that is if anyone has anything to hide which I very much doubt."

"Seems as though a boat has gone out this morning lookin' at the lines in sand."

"Oh that'ull be the kids, they have a row boat that they got from me, they love to go out there he continued, infact they are out there now according to their Gran Lizie for the day." "They also went out there yesterday too, all seven of them." Un-beknown to Mr. Winkle he had just given the thieves a vital piece of information.

"Err—Mr. Winkle can we rent a boat out here in town?, fancy a look at Gundaga Island I do." asked Nettles.

"Yep, you'll see an old wooden shack with the paint peeling off down by the stone pier, there you'll see a Captain Jeff his last name being Bobbleton but we all just call him Capt'n J."

Planks began to rub the stubble around his chin as Mr. Winkle bade them farewell.

"He seemed like a nice old guy, always good to know the locals" Nettles mused.

"Right, we need to see Capt'n Jeff about renting a boat for the day."

"One day should be enough I should think" said Razor. He too was thinking that he needed to shave his beard back a bit as he didn't like the feel or look of his stubble too. Grizzly!

All three of them had obviously not taken great care of themselves over the years. For one all were over weight, bellies bulging over belt buckles, their teeth very yellow and in Planks case some black too.

Dental hygiene had not been a priority with them. Bloodshot eyes indicating that they might have had too many late nights with a bottle of dark rum. Captain Jeff was in for a surprise when he would meet these out of town visitors!

As they approached the paint peeling shack a short stocky man with prescription glasses and a salt and pepper color close cut crew style of hair was messing about with some ropes that needed re-knotting.

"Mornin', would you by any chance be Capt'n Jeff?" asked Nettles.

"We spoke to a Barnabus Winkle on the beach not too long ago" added Razor.

"He did say that we could rent a boat for the day."

"I'm the man alright, medium sized boat do for you?" he asked as he shook hands with the trio noticing extremely dirty hands and fingernails.

"We plan to take a trip out to Gundaga Island, heard that there are many species of birds out there which we wouldn't mind seeing" lied Razor.

"Ornithologists, well welcome to Gundaga and all it has to offer which is quite a bit."

"No kiddin'" muttered Planks under his breath.

Walking down to the water after the necessary paper work had been filled out to see their boat Planks just had to ask under his breath "Orney whats', what did he mean Razor?"

"The study of birds you ninny" his frustrated partner told him, don't you know anything?"

"Well big fancy word it is and I ain't no scholar" Planks replied with annoyance.

"OK, this one do for you?" asked Capt'n J, 202-11P was the boats' registration number, how un-canny, what a coincidence too!

31

The engine putt-puttered then roared to life sending gurgling bubbles to the surface.

"Everybody on" said Capt'n J then he gave the boat a good push off from the stone pier. "Right, see you all later, you have the boat until tomorrow morning."

With that the thieves pulled away from the pier and out of the small harbor none of them wearing the life vests provided. Again they were breaking the law as they set out for Gundaga Island. Yes they too were on their way at last.

*   *   *

CHAPTER NINE

WITH PUPILE DILATED, EYES AS wide as saucers the seven brave cousins gingerly moved forward deeper into the cave. With more than one flash light this time it didn't appear to be as bad plus this was a much larger cave than the other ones were. Because of it's size the smell wasn't as bad either as more air was allowed to filter inside. About three minutes from entering the cave they all figured that they were quite a distance from the entrance, then a large opening appeared. In front of them there was a kind of rocky bent out circle with many rock shelves too.

"OK, let's split up a bit in this circle, I'm sure between us the bags should be easy to find" said Christian.

The flash lights bobbed up and down as they all searched for what would be a fantastic discovery and very soon. A squeaking noise came from above the kids' heads sending chills down their spines "BATS! shouted Sam, get down before they peck at our heads!"

"It's the light that they object to" wailed Catrin.

Whoosh as one flapped by then another and another all seven of them being struck with terror as they threw themselves to the sandy floor of the cave lying as flat as pancakes without any light.

"I bet dungeons were as black as this" Caleb said trying not to get sand in his mouth as he spoke. He had before the summer recess been learning about castles and their darker elements reserved for prisoners. The girls were extremely quiet at this point choked up with fear as they lay there not daring to move a muscle whilst the colony of bats with their red angry eyes which were like pools of fire hovered above the kids' heads.

"Wonder how long it will take them all to settle down, I am so scared" admitted Christian.

"We all are" a tearful Abbey said.

It did take quite some time before the many bats settled aloft again meaning that at least a little light could be shone up towards the rock shelf where the money should be, what an enticing moment it was for them all. Smudgy (Al Smear) and Pews had decided that it was about time to visit Gundaga again to see if their buddies had taken the scrolled message from the beach. A gaping hole in the sand confirmed that they had indeed taken the message. Now then are they on or making their way out to the island?

"Let's go and check out that place with boats for hire" suggested Pews.

"Good thinkin'" said his buddy Smudgy, "I can't wait for them to get back." "But wait, I thought that we were supposed to meet here before going out there to finalise our plans?" asked Smudgy.

"Just a feeling, but I wonder if something has gone wrong" Pews pondered. He struck a match to light up his cigarette. "Pity that we can't call them but as agreed by all of us phone calls can be traced and that we do not need. Then he took several inhalations of his cigarette the smoke coming down both of his nostrils.

"I see the van over there" Smudgy announced to Pews, *90012-3on, that's the plate alright he thought. At this point no one had suspected the van and the robbery as being one.

"Good thing that we changed that license plate" said Pews. "Buying us more time" then another cloud of blueish smoke surrounded him as he inhaled and exhaled.

"Afternoon gents, Jeff Bobbleton but call me Capt'n J as everyone else does, how may I help you?"

"Lookin' for two friends of ours" said Smudgy.

"Make that three as Smudgy here cannot count" an annoyed Pews corrected.

"I did rent a boat out to three guys only this morning, Nick Sharpe, Will Sting and a Woody Splinter, bringing it back tomorrow morning, said they were going bird spotting."

"Right then I guess we'll just have to stay at the motel in town here for the night, thanks for your help Capt'n J." And so with that off they went. Pews was the more clean cut guy of the five (apart from his bad habit of smoking) and was probably the most intelligent one too. The others made more followers than leaders though Razor could be a close second to Pews. Smudgy made the good messenger and driver of the gang but tended to get easily side tracked.

When they had rolled into town earlier on that afternoon in the rusted red car from the 1970's with all it's rattles and moaning chasis it caused more of a stare than a brand new shiny car with spoofed up wheels and a powerful noisy exhaust would have done!

"Where in the heck did you find this thing on wheels?" asked Pews to Smudgy.

"At the scrap yard, where else do you think I would go?" answered Smudgy quite indignantly.

*mirror needed.

"That figures coming from you, we have all this money and you buy this!"

"Not yet we don't" Smudgy said back, that being the most sensible thing that he had said in a long time.

The motel proved perfect, the room having a good view of the harbor so they could keep a good watch on the pier waiting for the other three of them to show up.

"I think that they will be back tonight" said Pews breaking a long silence.

"Yeh, you're probably right as where would they sleep out on that island?"

"Heard that there are lots of bats in them there caves that the island has" Pews added with a shudder.

"They won't sleep in caves we know that especially bat infested ones" grimaced Smudgy at the thought, definitely not! . . . .

*   *   *

CHAPTER TEN

CHRISTIANS' THUMB PRESSED DOWN ON the rubber button of the flash light immediately the welcoming beam of light a joy to them all. By using just the one flash light they hoped that it would not disturb the for now contented bats above their heads. Christian shone the light towards the ceiling of the cave, then down to where the rock shelf was. Much to their surprise there was more than one rock shelf within the circle.

"Look, he exclaimed, there is a plastic bag of some sort just to the left."

"Yes you're right!" an excited Caleb shouted back.

"Can we reach it?" asked Cole.

Sam moved forward with Cole whilst the girls stayed back in one place very much afraid should the bats attack again.

"If I stand on your shoulders Christian I think that I can reach it."

With help from Caleb and Cole Sam was hoisted up onto Christians' shoulders and keeping fairly well balanced managed to grab hold of the bag.

"Wow!, I think we have found what we came here for as this feels squishy like money in here" he squealed. Sure enough when the bag was opened up thousand dollar bills looked right back at them all and so many of them too.

"You mean we have found the stolen money?" Catrin blurted out excitedly.

"Eeek" Maddie shrieked.

"Let me see, let me see" Abbey noisily added.

"We need to find the rest if there is more" frothed Cole.

Atop Christians' shoulders again Sams' fingers groped for the rocky shelf inspite of the beam of light that was casting many shadows, probably too many.

"Dare we risk a bit more light?" he asked.

"Can sure try" Cole answered.

"OK, I see more up here several more and a metal box too" which turned out to be quite heavy but still had to be thrown down with the bags of money too to the waiting children.

"Look out, Jeromino" he yelled as everything hit the floor creating a dust cloud of sand, the metal box making a crater as it landed!

"Owch my shoulders are a bit sore" Christian said, "but it was well worth it.

"It has a lock on it but maybe we can pick it" disappointed as Caleb was. "Well not right now, let's get it to the mainland where the cops can deal with it."

"Good idea Christian" said Abbey as she wanted to get out of the creepy cave as fast as possible.

The five bags were not too heavy at all, it was just the metal case, but it not being overly large it was manageable between them.

"It has to have gold bars or something like that for it to be so heavy" Catrin puffed as she helped to carry it to the caves' entrance.

Thankfully the dreaded bats had stayed aloft inspite of the light much needed to find their way out, and there was the entrance in the near distance, how welcoming it sure looked to them all.

"Phew we got lucky there, we escaped the bats" said Maddie.

Space was going to be limited on the boat but the girls had offered to sit on top of the money! Suddenly everyone stopped dead in their tracks just a few feet from the mouth of the cave. A motor boat could be heard approaching the cove.

"Quick, get the binoculars out, let's see who this is" Christian kind of demanded the urgency in his voice apparent. "There are three men in the boat, I wonder if they are the bank thieves?"

"I wish I was with Lizie right now."

"Me too."

"And me."

All three girls said in turn frightened at the thought of what could happen next, would they get out and away in safety, would any of them get hurt?

Razor, Nettles and Planks had been in great anticipation as they made their way across the sea to Gundaga Island. Would they find the money which they truly thought belonged to them?, or would it be somewhere else? How they wished that they could contact Smudgy and Pews, things had really become messed up!

"That'ull be the kids boat over there" shouted Nettles above the noise of the engine, "we need to find them and quick."

They had already sailed around the island once and saw that the cove was the only way to and from the mainland to beach a boat.

"When we reach the beach, I want you Planks to go and grab them there oars outta the kids boat then they will be stuck HA HA!" laughed Razor.

"OK boss, sure thing" replied Planks as he waited for the boat to near the beach. Jumping off as he did it was like he had a set of springs attached to his feet as he made a mad dash over to Adventure, grabbing the oars as he did and swiftly placing them in their own boat. With that done the three of them now had to decide just which cave or trees up there on the cliff top the kids could be behind or in!

"Now I see that there are five caves here so I reckon that our dear Smudgy would have picked out one of these as he wouldn't climb all the way up there carrying bags too."

"So which one shall we start at?" asked Nettles. "We don't want to waste too much time going into each one."

"Nettles if we have to go into them all then that's just what we'll do!"

Planks really thought for a moment that the two of them were going to start a fight over which cave but good sense prevailed, well for now!

"I have a good idea" said Razor, "you Planks go in the first cave, you Nettles in the second cave, and I'll go into the third one, then after that we can go into the fourth and fifth cave together."

"Sounds good to me" replied Planks.

"Fine by me too" Nettles added and with that they split up to go into their designated cave.

*   *   *

CHAPTER ELEVEN

THE SEVEN COUSINS HAD BEEN watching all this action from the three men knowing full well that their oars had been placed inside the thieves' boat.

"We have to keep one step ahead of them" said Christian, "if I can make it down to their boat in readiness for a quick get-a-way you guys could grab our boat which we can tie up to theirs."

"Between us we can drag the money bags and case to put into our boat" stressed Caleb.

"This sounds very good guys as then they will be stranded on this island just waiting for the cops to come and arrest them" a half excited, half scared Maddie added.

"That was sure a smart thing to do before we all went into that fifth cave covering up our footprints lest they would have gone into that one first!" exclaimed Sam.

"You bet" they all chorused.

"Right, action, let's get going as they have all disappeared into the we know what" Christian smiled.

"Yep, bat infested."

HA! HA! chuckled the girls, serves them right!

Christian made a mad dash from the cave to the thieves boat whilst Cole made a bee line for Adventure. There he grabbed the rope and successfully tied it to the other boat, tightly knotted Christian could now think about starting the motor up in readiness. On cue Caleb Sam and the girls began the what seemed like the longest run of their lives, but in actuality they didn't have to run too far dragging the bags and that case as they did.

Half way down the beach a terrible sight met all their eyes, Planks and Nettles had come out of the first and second caves, these being the shorter ones of the five caves. Immediately they saw what was happening on the beach and with their stash!

"Hey you kids, yelled Nettles, where d'ya think you're going with all that? it belongs to us."

Cole was madly jumping up and down in the boat as Christian revved up the engine to it's hilt.

"C'mone you guys, run for your life, they have seen us."

"Hurry shouted Cole, they are starting to run after you!"

Dragging the bags and two carrying the metal case they were almost at the waters' edge when Maddie took a tumble with one of the bags.

"Maddie, get up and quick, they are closing in on you" a terrified Sam shouted from the top of his lungs. "Hurry, Hurry!"

The others made it to the waters' edge herding through the water like wild stallions on the move. With a quickness the bags and case were flung over the side of Adventure, um at this point I don't think any of them noticed the weight of the box!

"Maddie do hurry" they all yelled at her as she scrambled to her feet still clutching the bag of money.

Planks was closing in on her and fast too. He had once been a good runner in his youth, but being out of condition having not looked after himself he was beginning to feel the pace.

Maddie was also a good runner, luckily she had had the hindsight to tie up her waist length blonde hair so that it would not hinder her in her flight from the bank robber.

"C'mere you urchin of a kid" Planks snarled at her as she built up her speed to keep the narrowing distance between them. "You'll not git away from me" he said bearing his yellow and black teeth, his bloodshot eyes gleaming at her.

"No, no, you are not going to get me" and with that she flung herself at Adventure making it over the side with the money and one of her legs. Planks took hold of the other leg at the ankle, his grip so vice like she just couldn't shake him off. Christian by now was frantic almost wanting to spin the boat out of control and make circles. Without a word Caleb and Sam leaped out of the boat both taking an oar each with them ready to do war if need be. This horrible man was not going to take their beloved cousin with him as ransom!

They both swung at him with the oars hitting him in the back and chest making him stumble backwards into the water stunning him. Nettles seeing all this kept his distance and just watched in silence. Just at that moment Razor came out of the third cave to see the mayhem taking place. Making a dash for the scene he then realised that Planks was flat on his back in the waves.

"What the, blasted kids" he said as he shook his fist at the now speeding boat leaving the cove sending quite a wake as the kids fled!

"You're not done yet grizzled Nettles, there are still two more of our gang to get passed and they will be waiting for yer!" He doubted if they had even heard him but his hand gestures told the same story.

Christian had spun both boats around so sharply that all of them had gone flying side on and backwards almost to the point of going over-board.

Maddie stranded in the boat behind them had also taken a swoop backwards but her landing being a rather soft one as she landed on the money bags. Her face was all flushed as she trembled, all she could think about was the look on the mans' face and his red sausage like fingers wrapped around her ankle.

"I really need a big hug from someone right now she thought aloud, oh Lizie where are you?"

Planks was slowly coming to wondering just how he had been overcome by two kids. But it was them teal colored oars that got me, I didn't stand a chance he thought to himself. He also knew full well that Razor and Nettles would be furious at him for letting that girl with the long blonde hair get away when he almost had her.

"You bumbling idiot! exploded Razor, now they have got away with all that belongs to us." "How we really need to get in touch with Pews and Smudgy and what's more Planks we are totally stuck on this island, the only boat that we will be going back on will be a cop boat!"

Back at the motel Pews and Smudgy had become impatient with waiting for the others to return so they decided to take a walk along Gundaga beach.

Hopefully they would see a boat coming back and with all their stash too.

"Wonder if they hired a sloop?" a lazy idea of Smudgys' emerged.

"Why would they hire a sail boat when there are several small boats that would be adequate" reckoned Pews.

From the distance the two men could see a boat or is that two boats heading back to the mainland, heading straight for Gundaga beach!

"Yeh, our luck is in Smudgy, they are on their way back, whoa yes!"

"Yippee, our luck is in said Smudgy, soon all that money will be in our hands!"

*   *   *

CHAPTER TWELVE

"LOOKS AS THOUGH THERE IS help waiting for us on the beach" yelled out Christian over the din of the motor, outboards could be so noisy but better than rowing especially in an emergency.

Pews and Smudgy had made their way down to the waters' edge in readiness to help beach both boats.

"Hee hee, come to daddy" gleamed Pews.

"Wait, no stop, no I don't mean stop, turn around and get away from the beach" Cole shouted to Christian.

"Why?" he yelled back at his brother.

"Those two scruffy looking men I think they are part of the gang of thieves, remember that one of them was shouting something at us and doing all those hand gestures which suggested that there were two more of them back on the mainland."

"Yeh, I think Cole is right Christian" added Sam, Caleb agreeing whole heartedly with him.

"OK everybody hang on for dear life, Maddie hold on" and with some sign language she got the drift of what was about to happen.

Swoosh as the boat made a sharp swing to the right making the other boat swing out into a half circle coming closer to the beach than expected.

"Oh no, help, here we go again" Maddie exclaimed as she held on tightly her knuckles turning white. Catrin, Abbey and the others inspite of holding on had each in turn fallen backwards, their legs and feet now looking up at the sky! Maddie had taken a fall sideways and had somehow become lodged in between the seats so at least she was secure in the madly tossed about boat. Meanwhile Pews and Smudgy in horror of seeing the boats pull away from the beach had begun to wade into the water up to their waists not enjoying the chilled feel of it either.

"Where are you monsterous snot faced kids think you going?" a temper riddled Pews spat out.

"Away from you, you speccy four eyes idiot and the killer whale next to you" Christian blurted out as he continued to steer the boats at full throttle. He had decided to head for the safe sanctuary of the harbor speeding past Gundaga Point as he did.

It was late in the afternoon and Lizie had been anxious for the most part of it. Having not received the messages sent in the usual way from the kids out on the island to signify that all was well with them she thought that something must be wrong. Oh how I wish that the cell phones would work out there, you had to be very lucky if they did!

"Well I never" Lizie exclaimed as she looked through the binoculars for the twentieth time out to sea and the island. She saw two boats one being towed speeding across Gundaga Point and passed where Lizies' cottage stood. Maybe some kind folks who were out on the island with them offered them a ride back to save Christian rowing back. No that wasn't it she thought as she could see just her seven grand children and no one else, safe, but why were they going so fast and who owned the motor boat none of this making any sense at all.

"Camden, Kenzie we need to leave right away, come on to the car, we need to take a ride down to the wharf" and with that they sped out of the drive way. With the wild ride not quite over Christian came at full hilt into the harbor, the other six of them still in disarray but at least their feet were firmly back on the bottom of the boats!

"Slow down young man" shouted a fisherman at Christian.

"No wake in here sonny" said another.

"Hey what's the rush? the cops will give you a ticket for speeding."

"Call the cops please, this is an emergency." "We have the stolen money from the bank in Port Camjas and two of the thieves are on Gundaga beach probably making a dash to escape. The other three are stranded on Gundaga Island" he said quite out of breath with all the excitement and adrenalin rushing through his veins.

Lizie watched as the boats slowed in readiness to dock alongside the stone pier . . . . "What has happened?, you all look so frightened and worn out."

She grabbed hold of the rope that was thrown to her speedily tying it around the davit which was set into the stone pier, then repeating this with the other rope securing the boat totally. The second boat with Maddie still in it was tied up in the same way.

"Maddie, why are you in this boat on your own?" a curious Lizie asked.

"It's a long story Lizie, but first I need a really big hug from you, oh Lizie."

"Lizie you're not going to believe this" all the kids shouted at once. "We have the stolen money from the bank robbery the other day." Over the many voices Lizie couldn't make head nor tail of it all plus the police sirens were wailing in the background.

"Just what is in those five plastic bags?" asked Lizie.

"Money! money! and we think gold bars too in that case" Abbey yelled at the top of her voice.

"And the thieves, two of them are on the beach, the other three are stuck out on Gundaga Island" Sam added his blue eyes as wide as saucers.

Quite a crowd had gathered on the pier including the approaching police who were more than ready to find out just what was going on.

Spilling out from each of the adventurous seven the story began to make sense to the authorities.

As one officer worked on picking the lock to the case the others discovered the contents of the bags. Immediately more officers were dispatched throughout the town in the hopes of arresting Pews and Smudgy. Two police boats and one coast guard boat were prepared to leave destination Gundaga Island. With lights flashing, horns blaring they went out of the harbor leaving an enormous wake making the other moored boats bob up and down like corks in water.

"What in the world, rough seas in the harbor" went the surprised fishermen and started to make their way over to the gathered crowd on the pier.

Pews and Smudgy meanwhile had heard the sirens going off and had decided to hide out in the brown work van knowing that the kids would have by now given out information about them to the cops.

"This is not going very well for us Smudgy, but we could deny it all." "We could say that we have no connection with the robbery and those pesky kids are fibbing."

"Well let's just sidle out of town and now" suggested Smudgy as he started up the van. *90012-3 on quietly moved along the road but not for very long before it began to splutter and eventually the engine cutting out.

"Now what, Smudgy what have you done again?" he growled.

Smudgy tried desperately to re-start the van but it wasn't having it. Then his eyes fell upon the dials in the dash board the gas dial reading EMPTY! oh no . . . .!

*mirror needed.

*   *   *

CHAPTER THIRTEEN

Razor, Nettles and Planks had debated between themselves whether or not to run and go into hiding, but what was the use of doing that as there was no way off the island for them. The sirens beckoned getting forever closer, soon the police and coast guard would be beaching their boats, hand cuffs at the ready.

"Well we may as well just sit here on the beach to await our fate" a dismayed Nettles said.

"Yeah, Razor added, I still cannot believe that those kids got away like they did."

"They took me quite by surprise" a sopping wet Planks repeated, "them there oars didn't 'arf clobber me" he added rubbing his chest and side.

Seymore Keel, Officer Keel and Mack Herul, Officer Herul were the first boat to reach the beach quickly followed by Sar Dean Gill, Officer Gill and Robin A Bank, Officer Bank in the second police boat. The coast guard boat had begun to make it's way around the island manned by two boatswains, security officer Cliff Hanger and security officer Marcus A Schell making absolutely sure that there was no way that the three stranded thieves could make a get-a-way from the other side.

The four police officers approached Razor, Nettles and Planks with their weapons drawn.

"We are not armed" shouted Razor to them.

"Then put your hands up and keep them there" replied Officer Keel.

The three of them obeyed the order and as quick as a flash they were hand cuffed and swiftly taken down to the boats which were lolling in the gentle waves. Planks thought silently to himself that not too long ago he had been lolling in the waves overcome by two boys which he still found impossible to believe. Boy Razor and Nettles were sore at him, what a miserable failure I am. Breaking his silent thoughts he shouted out aloud "Nuthin's gon' right!"

"Yeah, you're right with that Planks, wonder how things have gone on for Pews and Smudgy back on the mainland" said Razor in front of the cops without realising that he had just done a grave misdeed to his accomplices.

Pews in his frustration lit up another cigarette engulfing himself in clouds of smoke much to the annoyance of Smudgy who was a non smoker.

"Remember said Smudgy, I was not the last person to drive this van, one of the others failed to keep an eye on the gas gauge." "Now we need to make our way over to the car and get outta 'ere" still disgusted with his mate and his bad habit, winding down the window for some gulps of fresh air.

"Guess you're right Smudgy sorry" and then took another huge puff on the cigarette.

The two of them pushed the van to the side of the road and as they did they noticed the police boats and the one coast guard boat returning lights and sirens all ablaze.

"They'll be docking in Gundaga very soon which means that Razor, Planks and Nettles have been arrested I should think" said Pews.

"Best get going" and with that the two of them made a dash for the old red car which was parked closer into town, nearer to the pier. Both of them were panting un-controllably not being used to running at all, their lungs screaming in agony back at them.

"Not much further" gasped Smudgy slowing down considerably.

Pews didn't respond as he was too out of breath and had sub-consciously decided to give up smoking.

Seeing the crowd gathered on the pier staying un-detected was key to make that great escape. Upon reaching the red car both men were in virtual collapse, neither one could utter a word as they gasped for oxygen. They simply had to get inside the car to stay out of sight which they managed but Pews complained that he was going dizzy and light headed.

"Get your head down then you'll be OK" barked Smudgy feeling rather good at telling Pews what to do for a change, his own breathing getting back to normal fairly quickly.

The police and coast guard boats were by now preparing to dock, their three prisoners looking as meek as lambs. Yes they would be going to jail, no future lay in store for them. Each one of the three were wondering silently about the where-a-bouts of Pews and Smudgy totally un-aware that they were actually looking at them from afar as they stood on the stone pier.

Smudgy turned the key in the ignition and the old car revved and roared to life. Clunking it into gear they quietly made their way out of Gundaga and were thinking of freedom.

Hans Grouper, Officer Grouper had been working on picking the lock to the metal box when mission accomplished the lid sprung open revealing several medium sized gold bars, their worth being in the millions at a rough guess.

"Wow, just look at those, what a find he said to his partner, those kids did well to carry this back between them."

The gold bars were quite dazzling to the eye in the evening sun as all the kids looked at them in total dis-belief.

Then another sight met all their eyes, the three scruffy men from the island who were being escorted to the waiting squad cars.

Planks and Maddies' eyes met and locked in for a few seconds as he passed by her, a glutteral growl rising up from his throat.

"I'll git you one day missey."

"No you won't because you are going to jail, your fingers are like fat red sausages and your teeth are all yellow and black" she yelled back at him. All she heard was "grr" as he was put into one of the police cars.

"Did you see how all three of them looked at us" said Christian.

"Almost like they were taking mental pictures of us in their minds" Caleb hinted.

"Do you really think that one day they might come after us?" asked Catrin.

"You bet replied Sam, after what we took from them."

"I do like the look of those gold bars, so shiny, and all that money too" Abbey motioned as she walked over to where the money bags sat on the pier. Officer Keel made his way over to the kids and Lizie as the cars sped away to the police station.

"I cannot thank you all enough, you are really small town heroes" he said.

"We would do it all over again if we had to" they all chimed.

"It was really Camden and Kenzie who started it all as they were the ones to find the message written by Smudgy" a proud Christian said as he looked directly into Officer Keels' eyes.

"Smudgy, said the officer, would he be one of the two still out there, one of the men said that there were two more on the mainland." "Now I wonder just where they are?"

"Probably making a get-a-way—as we speak."

"Y'know kid you are so right, but we'll get them."

Pews and Smudgy knew that they had been very lucky to get out of Gundaga as the place was swarming with cops.

"If we take our time we won't draw attention to us, but in the meantime we are stone cold broke, um robbing another bank is not an option" said Pews.

"What about trying to get one of them kids as ransom" Smudgy suggested.

"It's really not safe at present or in the near future to return to Gundaga, let it lapse for a few months."

After a long pause Pews got a glint in his eye.

"There is always that Mr. Winkle guy too."

"Good thinkin' Pews, good point!"

*   *   *

CHAPTER FOURTEEN

I N ALL THE EXCITEMENT NO one had taken particular interest in the gathering media from F.I.S.H. TV Network who had got all the events on their news reel. Red hot, fresh off the press to be aired that night and not to mention the interviews that would follow over the next few days of the towns' newly appointed heroes.

"All this excitement is making my head spinny" said Lizie who was feeling extremely proud of all of all of her grand children, "just what will your parents think of all this?"

"Oh yeh, I'd forgotten all about them confessed Cole, anyone else think that too?" he asked.

One by one they all had to say that because of the busy events they too had not thought of them, not even to call them. But they will understand once they see us all on TV.

The gathered crowd and the fishermen began to wonder off in different directions but not before congratulating all of the children for their fine efforts.

"We will look out for you all on the TV tonight" was the general theme.

After piling into Lizies' vehicle and on the approach to the cottage a familiar figure emerged, Mr. Winkle had been waiting for them to return.

"Well Hello mi little 'uns, mi little 'eros I hear" said the elderly man.

"Mr. Winkle" they all squealed as they jumped out of the SUV once it had stopped. They all ran up to him with ready embraces, arms to be flung about him.

"Brace yourself Mr. Winkle like I do" laughed Lizie which he did!

Mr. Winkle was so happy that they were all safe, but at the back of his mind the nagging thought that there were still two more thieves out there, probably not in Gundaga but that could easily change too he thought.

Once inside the stone cottage Lizie set about to prepare the evening meal inviting Mr. Winkle to stay too which he readily accepted.

The delicious smell of home made chicken pot pie soon filled the kitchen. What a lovely meal they were about to have and then watch the early evening news afterwards.

"Lizie, how did you know that chicken pot pie, mashed potatoes and gravy is my favorite as he tucked into it fork full after fork full. Yum yum!

The F.I.S.H. network blared onto the TV screen, "nine children local heroes escaping capture out on Gundaga Island, bringing the millions worth of money and gold bars back to the mainland for the police to deal with. Risking everything in their get-a-way boat towing their own boat behind, one girl in it with the money bags. One of the men almost got her but two of the boys set upon him with the oars knocking him backwards into the water. These kids are truly very brave and risked everything all in the cause of justice."

Pictures of the pier flashed onto the screen as the bulletin continued, the kids seeing themselves on TV for the first time.

"Yikes, look at us" shouted Caleb.

"Wow we sure do look good eh" said Sam.

"We sure do" answered his sister.

"Looking much better than those men horrible as they are with the bad teeth" Catrin had to say.

"Look Kenzie, Camden you are on TV" an exhilarated Lizie said.

"And if it wasn't for the younger two of the children who by accident dug up the secret message from a guy named Smudgy then none of this would have happened." "They would have got away with it" said the newscaster Sebastian Carp. "We will be interviewing the heroes over the next day or so too."

"Did anyone notice the registration on the hired boat?" asked Christian, 202-11P.

"Not really" replied the others, "but I would bet that you would need a mirror, it must read something of significance!"

"You are right as it does" Christian answered.

"Like what?"

"Maddie, do you have your mirror handy?"

"Sure do cousin."

Christian wrote the registration down on a piece of paper and with the mirror all was revealed, 911-SOS!

"Wonder if Mr. Jeff Bobbleton knows this, you know Capt'n J, 'um."

"Christian, how did you figure that out without a mirror?, you are so a hero and smart too" an admiring sister of his had to say making him blush up.

"I love you brother."

"And I love you too Catrin."

Sure enough the following morning whilst breakfast was yet again being devoured the phone began to ring off the hook.

"That will be the reporters announced Lizie, wanting to set up a time when to come over to interview you all." She was of course right and made the necessary arrangements for the two reporters to visit later on that day, they being with the F.I.S.H. Network.

On that same morning arrangements had been made with the C.O.D.D. Network to interview them all at eleven o'clock and right on cue there was a knock at the door.

"The reporters are here" said Lizie.

"Hello there she said as she answered the door, I see that you are setting up the equipment for the interview."

"Yes ma'am" the man replied, he being a Mr. Herr Rings and his colleague a Mr. Gill Scaler.

"Welcome, do come in and meet the heroes" Lizie said. "They are still trying to believe that it all happened."

One by one they all introduced themselves and proceeded to go outside to start the interview which would be televised on the news later that night. Mr. Rings and Mr. Scaler were fascinated to hear all about how the adventure began and then the rescue of the stolen goods. Piece by piece it all un-folded.

"Wow, you have all been so brave, did you at anytime become scared for your lives? asked Mr. Rings.

"Yeah, when the bats attacked us in the cave as we were trying to get the money bags, y'see Caleb continued the bats did not like the light from our flash lights."

"And when the man with the red sausage fingers grabbed hold of my ankle, I really thought that he had truly got me, until Sam and Caleb came to the rescue that is" Maddie said excitedly.

"We grabbed the oars and we both went for him, knocking him down into the water, he was totally stunned" added Sam.

Kenzie and Camden had their share of things to tell to the reporters, explaining how whilst digging around in the sand they had come across the metal box which contained the message from Smudgy.

"So you see Abbey continued, they were actually the ones to start all of this."

"We are so clever" said Kenzie to Camden and gave him a big hug.

"It bothers me that there are still two more of them out there who may come after us at any time, we did rather botch up their plans" commented Christian.

Feeling satisfied that they had a good story to air later on that night Herr Rings and Gill Scaler bade them all a good farewell for now. Should they need to return for any more information then that would be OK too.

"Yes, of course, that would be fine" answered Lizie as she closed the door after they had left.

The F.I.S.H. Network arrived as planned in the afternoon with an eager Roger Jolley and a Skip Kipper to hear the story from the kids. So once again they repeated their bit of the adventure including the scariest moments too.

"Bet you kids were terrified?" Roger Jolley half asked, half stated.

"I thought that my heart was going to leap out of my chest!" Cole added.

An hour or so later, feeling that they too had a great story to air Mr. Jolley and Mr. Kipper thanked them all and went on to their next assignment.

Mr. Winkle had shown up at the cottage and had sat back to listen to the saga as it un-folded. He was feeling mighty proud of these little 'uns as he referred to them. He had also been giving some great thought into adopting a puppy from the local humane society and began to ask them all what they thought of the idea.

"Y'see mi little 'uns I kind of get lonesome sometimes now that I don't get out on the sea as much if at all and with mi dear Ethel gone." "I think it would be good for me to have something to look after and a companion too" he stressed.

"I think it's a wonderful idea Mr. Winkle" said Maddie who herself was very fond of dogs, especially puppies!

"What would you call it?" asked Catrin.

"Ooh, I don't quite know little 'un, depends what it will look like and then pick a name to suit it."

"Can we come with you?" asked Kenzie, her brown eyes as wide as chocolate drops.

"All of us" Camden shouted at the top of his voice.

"Of course you all can come, Lizie too" he replied at the top of his voice.

"OK then it's settled, shall we all go tomorrow, or is that too soon?" Lizie asked. "They really have only a short time left here with me then they will be going back home again."

"Tomorrow will be fine" he said with an excited gleam in his one eye.

"Mr. Winkle, you are the best" Abbey said as she gave him a big hug.

"Yes you are they all chanted in unison, they sure have a good friend in this elderly man.

*   *   *

CHAPTER FIFTEEN

IT HAD BEEN SO MUCH fun the previous night to watch the televised interview of them all and at one point Mr. Winkle could be seen sitting off to the side just listening.

As dawn broke one by one they all came out of their blissful sleep but stayed snuggled down in their sleeping bags, thinking and talking of all the events of the last few days when they had launched Adventure.

It was overcast outside even though rain wasn't in the forecast. The waves made a soothing sound as they broke gently on the beach below. Today their boat would need storing in Lizies' shed until their next visit which they hoped would be well before next summer.

"I bet Mr. Winkle has some good stories to tell of the sea and old myth tales too" a sleepy Cole said.

"It would be great to visit Gundaga Island with Mr. Winkle and even Port Camjas where he is from" an equally sleepy Sam added.

"I bet he could teach us some of those songs, sea shanties that we could sing along too our hearts content" a smiling Maddie said with a yawn.

Kenzie made her way over to Maddies' sleeping bag and began to climb in with her sister to snuggle which they did, both disappearing under the cover.

All this chatter amongst them had continued from both bedrooms through the open doors but at a louder decibell.

"I don't hear Lizies' gong yet, but it could go off at any moment now" Christian suggested.

"Get ready" yelled Caleb and he too disappeared under his sleeping bag.

Sure enough and without a moment to spare BANG BANG BANG! went the dreaded gong, once again announcing that breakfast was ready.

Now everyone had disappeared under their sleeping bags, who would be the first to emerge?

As the awful clanging noise died down heads appeared again, then the race was on, who would be first at the breakfast table?

"Good morning Lizie" shouted Christian then the others joined him Kenzie being extra careful not to collide with the racket making metal.

"Mr. Winkle is coming around about ten o'clock" Lizie reminded them and to be ready was the cue.

"Yappity Yap," "Woof Woof" was the incredible noise down at the humane society in Gundaga town, so many puppies and dogs to choose from. Maddie was in her element and if she could would have taken them all with her!

"All of them look adorable" Abbey said to Catrin.

"Yes they do" she replied to her cousin as she tightened the elastics holding her shoulder length blonde hair in two pig tails.

As Mr. Winkle and Lizie walked through the kennels he noticed a small white puppy which was probably just three months old looking all forlorn, not even making a sound as the others carried on barking, wagging their tails to a frenzy. It's big blue eyes just stared back at Mr. Winkle but he did notice a faint wag of it's little tail.

As he continued to walk around he couldn't forget the white puppy that was somehow implanted in his brain.

"Lizie, they are all in need of a good home and I love them all, but that little white puppy just stole mi 'eart an' I thinks it's going to be that one."

"Gosh Mr. Winkle, he is so cute and will keep you busy with the house training and all that comes with the responsibilities of looking after one so little."

"Let's tell mi little 'uns eh."

This idea of Mr. Winkles had obviously been on his mind as he had already bought all the necessary things needed for the doggy world. Just the paper work, license and fees needed to be dealt with which took up some time to do. Everyone was fussing over the puppy once released from her cage. The boys had petted her being non plussed, but the girls were cooing and ahh'ing over her like mother hens keeping eggs warm! Abbeys' cute little nose with it's freckles buried itself in the lovely soft fur their eyes being of a similar bright blue color.

"Gee, I want one" she said but then they had their most loyal and precious Babe who would be making an entrance tomorrow with his woofing! Apparently their parents were coming over earlier because of all that had gone on cutting the vacation short by a couple of days. Lizie kind of knew that the kids (well at least the girls) would want to spend the afternoon at Mr. Winkles' place so she ordered four large pizzas for lunch which she picked up in town before heading back to the cottage.

There were some phone messages for Lizie, actually quite a few so one by one after lunch and after dispatching the girls at Mr. Winkles' place she busied herself with them.

Officer Keel wanted to come over and see her with the children and jokingly with no arrests! Local businesses were also offering rewards for all nine heroes. The bank that was robbed having received their stolen money and gold bars back wanted to offer them all a reward too.

"My oh my" thought Lizie aloud, "we didn't expect all this, wait until they all hear of this."

The boys had gone down to the beach for their final afternoon, Adventure turned up-side down fixed to wooden stakes in the sand which they needed to put into Lizies' shed by the end of the day.

"Well we sure did have an adventure, didn't we?" stated and asked Sam. "What a fantastic time and heroes too."

Camden had decided to stay with the older ones for a change, besides his sand digging buddie Kenzie had gone with the girls to fuss over the new white puppy.

"I wonder what name Mr. Winkle will give to her?" asked one.

"Don't know, but let him do that because remember when we were asking him what name would be good for our boat, he saying that it would be better if we thought up a name ourselves and not him for better good luck, so I guess the same applies" said Christian.

"Yeah, maybe she won't poop inside the house for him!" Cole said matter of factly.

"Um, well there's bound to be accidents" said Sam who wasn't referring to Babe in the least.

Officer Keel came over that same afternoon explaining that the police force wanted to hold a ceremony at the local town hall in the near future to award them badges for bravery and courage.

The bank in Port Camjas were offering to open banking accounts at any bank of their parents choosing for the minors with a deposit of $5,000 in each. What a grand reward indeed!

*   *   *

CHAPTER SIXTEEN

PACKING UP TO LEAVE THE next day was not nearly as much fun as it had been packing to go to Lizies' place. Somberly they all collected their things together and began to stuff them in their canvas bags.

"So this is our last night here for a while" Sam said miserably.

"I know" Caleb said equally as miserable as Sam.

"Cheer up Christian gestered, we will be back before you know it."

"Remember we have Lizie and our boat to take care of" Cole added.

"Lizie promised that she would come and see us all at home and maybe she will bring Mr. Winkle and his new puppy too" Abbey shouted from the girls room.

"Did he give the puppy a name?" asked Kenzie.

"Yes he did, don't you remember he has called her Daisy Mae" Catrin reminded Kenzie.

"Ohh, OK" she said and began to cuddle her blanky.

Silence embraced the cottage as everyone began to fall asleep after what seemed like another busy day. It began to rain during the night with an up-scale breeze which blew the drapes around quite a bit but no one heard a thing, how about that!

Minus the gong breakfast was the usual affair though it was scrambled eggs nice and fluffy for everyone with toast, milk and cranberry juice too. The familiar sound of "woof woof woof" was getting closer to the cottage.

"Babe" shouted Sam and Abbey at the tops of their voices estatic to hear him and momentarily see him as he would indeed come bounding in through the open door. The sleek black dog with orange tips over his eyes came lolloping in making headway for Sam and Abbey, then the rest of the kids Lizie too. Lizie was very fond of Babe and loved him like her own.

Becca and Craig came into the kitchen, Sam and Abbeys' mom and dad to hugs and kisses all round.

"Ah we are so glad to see you kids, what an adventure you have all had" said their dad, "Lizie how have you coped with everything?" Becca asked her mom.

"You know me, do the best I can, but they did rather surprise me with all the goings on and all those TV people and cops" Lizie replied.

"You just have to see our boat which we called "Adventure," Mr. Winkle let us have it" Abbey yelled with excitement.

"Hello" shouted another voice from the doorway, "Mommy" yelled Kenzie and Maddie as their mom Ruth came into the kitchen too.

"My girls, how are you, and mom how are you too?" she asked.

The two girls got up so quickly that their chairs took a slip slide narrowly missing the infamous gong!

With all the greetings, hugs and excitement Babe decided to do his doggy yodeling nose in the air, all he needed was a cliff top and a full moon to pass off as a wolf in a portrait!

Honk, Parp, Honk echoed from outside.

"Mom's here" the 5'cs said out loud and ran outside to meet her and the twins Jarid and James.

"How are you all doing after all the events that have been going on?" their mom Rachael asked, ooh I am so glad to see you all, I have missed you all so much and the danger that you were in, how are the others?"

She followed them all inside hands full with the twins to greet everyone else.

"Good Lord" said Craig as he had gone outside to the shed with Sam to see the boat.

"Well we were pretty limited for paint colors and seeing that we all couldn't agree on anything specific this is what we decided to do and at least it's unique right dad."

"I guess so" said Craig laughing but enjoying the in-geniousness of it all.

Knock, Knock came the sound from the door of the cottage then a familiar face poked around the door. "It's only me, Mr. Winkle."

"Come on in, come and meet the childrens' parents."

"I would like you all to meet Mr. Barnabus Winkle my neighbor and friend and a good friend to all of your children, he was the very kind person who gave them a row boat."

"Hello" Mr. Winkle came the chorus.

"Hello, nice to meet you all too, them little 'uns are something so special, I'll bet you're so proud of 'em, they sure have had an adventure, I do hope that they will all be back sooner than next summer."

"They will but in the meantime I plan to go and see them and I hope that you would like to ride back with me, bring Daisy Mae too" Lizie added.

"I would like that very much if that's OK with everyone else too."

"Mr. Winkle, of course it is" added the three daughters of Lizie the three R's.

Much to Lizies' delight her daughters and son-in-law had stayed on to listen to the wild tales of Gundaga Island and the constant chatter coming from all corners. The beach made the perfect place to relax and enjoy part of the day but soon they would all have to leave, leaving Gran Lizie somewhat sad, but she realized that she needed to re-charge her batteries so to speak.

"I promise to look after "Adventure" for you, maybe take up a little rowing for myself, cannot get old with all you grand-children around now can I" she said laughingly.

"Next time we are out here Becca said "let's all go out to the island, hire a motor boat from Cap'n J, yeh that would work."

"Yeah, I would love to go out there, even the caves too" replied Ruth expecting retaliation from the kids concerning those dreaded bats, but not one word was said!

Nine bags were reluctantly thrown into and between the three vehicles ready for the off. Goodbyes and see you soon were exchanged between all and then it was really time to leave. Tears welled up in Lizies' eyes but she was determined that none would show in front of everyone, heck they could flow later she thought.

"Remember to text and send e-mails too when you all can as I will and take care my little ones "she said as she waved bye for now to them.

And above all the clamour of we love you and see you soon the unmistakable woof woof woofing could be heard from non other than Babe the dog!

A FEW WEEKS LATER TOWARDS THE end of the summer a ceremony was held, the kids each receiving a medal of honor for bravery, courage and honesty which took place in Gundagas' town hall with Officer Keel officiating. Other local businesses had also offered them lots of specials from free ice cream for the next two years to free hair cuts for the boys, free pedicures for the girls for the next two years. They would also be eating alot of pizza!

It turns out that Pews used to work at the bank that they robbed in Port Camjas, having a good knowledge of where everything was. Surveillance cameras, alarms, codes and most importantly just what was in the safe and the personnel deposit boxes. By going into the bank very early in the morning disguised as work men to do repairs (he had made duplicate copies of all the keys needed) it made the robbery quite easy for them all. So with zero alarms not going off, no one detected that anything was wrong.

The three of them Razor, Planks and Nettles each received life sentences, they all having more than one attempted robbery associated with their names. The police and FBI still remain confident that the other two will soon be caught, Pews and Smudgy, just a matter of time . . . .

Lizies' grand children soon got over the shock and excitement of their summer adventure in Gundaga. Always a good story to tell from now on!

Back in their routines using gadgets of the hi-tech age, computers, cell phones, i-pods etc, things they had not bothered with all summer long. They had been having too much fun (before the robbery adventure) discovering things outside, being with nature, building tree houses and bird spotting too!

The noise of the school buses filled the morning air, kids all waiting to be picked up for the start of yet another school year. What a summer it had been.

*   *   *

ABOUT THE AUTHOR

Elizabeth Holland was born and raised on a farm in Lancashire, England. One of her goals in life was to write a fictitious adventure book for children but with real life theme. The child characters in the story being her actual grandchildren, the parents her daughters and son-in-law.

She has also lived in Australia and now resides in Ohio on the shores of Lake Erie. This is her first book.